For more than forty years,
Yearling has been the leading name
in classic and award-winning literature
for young readers.

Yearling books feature children's
favorite authors and characters,
providing dynamic stories of adventure,
humor, history, mystery, and fantasy.

Trust Yearling paperbacks to entertain,
inspire, and promote the love of reading
in all children.

OTHER YEARLING BOOKS YOU WILL ENJOY

Molly McGinty Has a Really Good Day

Gary Paulsen

A YEARLING BOOK

This is for Pat, Ann and Irene

Published by Yearling, an imprint of Random House Children's Books
a division of Random House, Inc., New York

Visit us on the Web! www.randomhouse.com/kids

Educators and librarians, for a variety of teaching tools, visit us at
www.randomhouse.com/teachers

ISBN: 0-440-41482-2

Reprinted by arrangement with Wendy Lamb Books

Printed in the United States of America

February 2006

10 9 8 7 6 5 4

OPM

Foreword

Most of my books have boys as main characters. There are exceptions: *The Monument*, *Nightjohn*, *The Night the White Deer Died* and *Sisters* were written about girls, and, I hope, in girls' voices. But much of what I write is about boys, because I was a boy and I did boy things—still do, since I'm what might be called an old boy.

But stories come from where they come from, and humor lives where it wants to live, and at least half the time it lives with girls.

And so this story of Molly, who is based on a girl who told me about her three-ring binder organizational system.

Chapter One

Organizing your day for maximum productivity is an art.

—*Molly's notebook*

"Don't you think Sparkleberry lipstick would be a good idea, cookie?"

Molly McGinty looked up at her grandmother from the math notes covering her desk and took a deep calming breath to prepare herself for the day ahead: Senior Citizens' Day at Our Lady of Mercy Middle School.

Molly had been sitting at the desk in her bedroom since five-thirty that morning trying to quiz herself on math formulas, or was it formulae (another thing

1

to look up). Her grandmother had been awake just as long, constantly interrupting.

"All I'm saying, doll, is that you might want to add a little jazz to your image. I mean, you are in the sixth grade now and it might be a good thing to . . . well, have some fun with your look." Irene Flynn looked at her granddaughter critically from her place before the mirror as she added yet another string of beads to her own glittering neck.

Yes, Molly reflected, Irene would think more sparkle was in order, considering her own "ensemble" that day, chosen in honor of her unbroken attendance record at the annual Senior Citizens' Day. Irene hadn't missed an opportunity to visit Molly's school since kindergarten. Sometimes Molly dreamt about the visits, all six of them. The dreams were always nightmares.

"Now that we're attending social functions together, call me Irene," Molly's grandmother had instructed her when she first began to attend school events. "I'm on a first-name basis with all my dearest friends."

That day Irene had already been talked out of the

2

hat with the feather. Molly had successfully argued that it would block the view of the blackboard for anyone unlucky enough to be seated within eight rows behind her. But Irene could not be persuaded that purple suede jeans were a bit loud for a school day.

"The salesgirl said *all* the kids were wearing these." Irene had pivoted in front of the mirror, admiring her new clothes. Molly hadn't known whether to tell her grandmother that she was far from being a kid, that Our Lady had a uniform-only dress code or that she'd been victimized by a sales-lady working on commission.

Molly sighed and turned back to concentrate on the math notes she'd borrowed. She'd fallen asleep at her desk the night before, resting her head on the pile of textbooks, index cards, other kids' illegible class notes and, apparently, her pencil—if the groove in her cheek that spelled out TICONDEROGA NO. 2 was any indication.

Not only was she facing perhaps the most brutal math test ever given and an entire day at school with Irene in tow, but the day before, Molly had lost her notebook.

Her Notebook that Contained Everything She Needed to Live.

Molly McGinty was organized. Very organized. Exceedingly organized. Everyone knew that about her. And the key to her organization was a multi-pocketed three-ring binder that she carried everywhere.

She had spent countless hours straightening and rearranging her notebook, getting it just so—no, getting it perfect. Molly's notebook wasn't just a place to keep paper and to put work sheets: it was a repository for valuable information.

She kept her homework in the school section (every class in a different-colored folder, of course) along with a cross-referenced listing of test schedules and the due dates of large projects and important papers. She was especially proud of her system for keeping track of when to return library books, a structured grid laid out by date and time of day. Two years earlier she had been reading a book about the Wright brothers and their first flight at Kitty Hawk that contained an old photo showing the inside of the shack the men lived in while getting ready for the first powered flight. On the wall of the shack was a wooden rack full of eggs, which they ate for breakfast. The book said that each egg was numbered in order of freshness so that the oldest egg could be eaten first.

Molly had nearly cried; she understood the Wright brothers perfectly and knew, *knew*, that their organizational abilities were the primary reason there were airplanes today. The Wright brothers probably had three-ring binders.

Molly's address book was in the social section of the binder. She included pertinent information about her friends: phone numbers, e-mail addresses, birth dates (including a special notation to avoid Kevin Spencer's birthday parties, where the combination of carrot cake, chocolate frosting and Neapolitan ice cream was a given and where on one occasion somebody had made the frosting with laxative as a primary ingredient), pets (type, size and general level of friendliness, with a jotted reminder to steer clear of the D'Agostinos' slobbery Great Dane, Caesar, who might or might not have eaten a cat), siblings (age and likelihood to be annoying during sleepovers, with a highlighted, double-underlined postscript to skip Patty Schumacher's house until the twins were done teething because they bit like Tasmanian devils and probably had not had their shots), and favorite subjects, for the organization of future study groups prior to final exams.

Lunch tickets were tucked into a zippered plastic pocket along with bus tokens and extra quarters for emergency phone calls, although Molly had never actually faced an emergency where a phone call would have helped, unless you counted the time Nicholas O'Connor set his hair on fire to show off for Kimberly Klein, and then the fire was well out before the fire department got to the bus. Still, she felt comforted knowing she was prepared.

The notebook also contained a family section, with a color-coded calendar so she'd know when to remind her grandmother to pay the bills. Molly had come up with that particular strategy after having taken phone messages from a number of bill collectors. Regardless of Irene's determination to look upon those two weeks without water and electricity as an urban adventure, Molly had not enjoyed bathing by candlelight with two-liter bottles of natural springwater heated, or rather slightly warmed, in a pan held over a butane lighter.

Molly's grandmother was a talent agent specializing in animal clients. ("Do you realize, sugar, that last month's entire mortgage was paid for by Dizzy the dog?" Irene had recently boasted. Dizzy was Irene's favorite, a three-year-old border collie who had landed the enviable role of spokesdog for the largest bank chain in a three-state area.)

Irene's unusual career explained, at least to Irene, why their home was in a constant state of upset. She claimed that she couldn't be on top of things at both her house and her business. Her creative juices would desert her if she was too regimented.

Apparently, her creativity was also threatened by paying bills on time, dressing sedately and dusting.

Molly had a schedule for housecleaning, too, in her lost notebook, immediately before the grocery list, the pager number of the emergency plumber and the list of her and Irene's doctor and dentist appointments for the next year.

Molly reluctantly dragged her thoughts from her lost data and watched Irene fluff her hair.

"Irene, did I already ask you if you'd seen my notebook?"

"Notebook? Hmmm . . . no, I haven't seen it today. But if you had a good bag, pet, a really smart purse, you'd never misplace anything. See . . . I can keep everything I need in my shoulder bag and, being basic black, it goes with everything I own!"

Irene triumphantly dragged her purse to the middle of the room. It was the approximate weight and size of a Marine Corps duffel bag. She hadn't been able to actually lift the purse for weeks now— ever since she'd ordered the miniature chess set from the Shopping Channel, the one-of-a-kind set with the pieces carved to represent the two teams who played in the 1991 World Series.

"You never know, angel," Irene had cooed when the chess set arrived in the mail. "This stuff could be worth a fortune someday to serious baseball memorabilia collectors. That series marked the start of the Atlanta Braves' emergence in the nineties."

Just as Molly began to worry that she would

be saddled with her grandmother's bag all day, she heard the kitchen door open downstairs.

She took a deep breath and braced herself for the invasion of the Marys.

Mary Margaret Blake, Mary Pat Montgomery and Mary Bridget Sheehan burst through Molly's bedroom door in a blur of navy blue plaid school uniforms.

"Hi, Molly."

"Hi, Molly."

"Hi, Molly."

"Mary Margaret. Mary Pat. Mary Bridget. Have any of you seen my notebook?"

Molly and the Marys had spent their school days together since kindergarten and rode on the same bus because they lived in four houses in a row on their street. At least one of the Marys was in every one of Molly's classes.

"Good morning, Mary Margaret—" Irene started.

"Mary Pat."

"Whatever."

"Excuse me, but we were trying to figure out if anyone had seen my notebook," Molly reminded everyone.

"Sweetie, you're going to have to learn how to go with the flow. It's the secret of life," Irene said.

"I thought you said the secret of life was having the right shoe for every occasion." Mary Bridget gazed doubtfully at her own scuffed loafers.

"No, the secret of life is going with the flow," Irene said firmly. "But you can never have enough shoes—that's true. I think you mixed up what I said, Mary Pat."

"Mary Bridget."

"Whatever."

"About my notebook . . ."

The oven timer rang at that moment and Irene dashed downstairs to the kitchen, calling, "Breakfast is ready."

Molly took another deep breath. Before the day was over, she was sure she'd have to hyperventilate just to get enough air to stay calm.

"Mary Margaret. Mary Pat. Mary Bridget. As you know, my notebook disappeared yesterday and I *still* can't find it." Molly paused, waiting for the full impact of her words to sink in.

Mary Pat turned pale, Mary Bridget let out a

small squeak of horror and Mary Margaret sat down hard on the bed.

"Oh, Mol . . . that's, well . . . that's just about the worst thing I ever heard. I was just sure the notebook would have turned up before school this morning." Mary Bridget looked as if she might actually burst into tears.

Mary Pat said carefully, "You had it yesterday in science. I know because I asked if I could look at that laminated periodic table of elements you have. But," she quickly added, "I gave it back to you. I did. I know I did." She looked frantically at the other Marys for support. They nodded vigorously.

"I've retraced my steps," Molly said as she began to pace. The Marys sat silently, barely breathing, only their eyes moving as they watched Molly walk back and forth.

"And I know that I brought my notebook home. I clearly remember setting it down by the back door when I got home from school yesterday. It was a Thursday, so that means I had to bring the empty garbage cans back to the garage."

The Marys nodded solemnly. Being neighbors, they had trash collection on the same day.

"But"—Molly wheeled around to face them—"when I returned to the house, before I could check off 'return cans to garage' on my Thursday to-do list, I got distracted. You know Irene fixes Mrs. Fritz's hair in our kitchen every Thursday before bingo."

"How's she doing?" Mary Margaret interrupted. "My great-uncle Charlie told me Mrs. Fritz has the most bingo wins at the weekly sixty-and-over game in the church basement. Great-uncle Charlie says that everyone swears that her good luck is because your grandmother does her hair every week. Maybe"—she looked thoughtful—"we should ask her to do *our* hair before big tests and things. Maybe Mrs. Flynn has the lucky touch."

Molly crossed her arms in front of her chest and tapped her foot impatiently. "That's not the point, Mary Margaret. The fact that my notebook has been missing for"—she checked her watch—"sixteen hours, seventeen minutes and four, no, five seconds now is the point."

Before the Marys could respond, Irene swept into

Molly's room, balancing a couple of plates on a tray.

Molly sniffed suspiciously. "What are you eating, Irene?"

"Orange roughy."

"I thought we agreed that you wouldn't eat fish for breakfast anymore."

"But tootsie, fish is brain food. And I need all the brainpower I can get today, considering I'm a schoolgirl again. Besides, it's not like that time we tried sardines and cereal—this is much more conventional. Have some fish, girls. I made enough for everyone. Here, try a bite, Mary Bridget."

"Mary Margaret."

"Whatever."

The Marys and Irene sat together on Molly's bed, oohing and aahhing over the perceived benefits of unadulterated protein to start the day. Molly's notebook crisis was forgotten. Molly shuddered at the idea of fish fillets at 7:35 in the morning and remembered with a jolt why she had suppressed the memory of the sardines and Frosted Flakes her grandmother had served as an experiment. The experiment was based on eating things solely for their nutritional value, and Irene swore that together, Frosted Flakes and sardines in vegetable oil contained everything necessary to support life.

"Okay, people. We need to concentrate, to focus on the important task at hand," Molly began, hoping that by sounding determined, she might rally her easily distracted forces and find her notebook before her entire day was ruined due to a lack of preparation and widespread fundamental uncertainty.

"That notebook is the single most important thing I own, and I depend on the information in it for every aspect of my life. I can't focus without it. My timing, for instance, is completely off. Timing . . . wait, there's something we're forgetting, something . . ."

Molly frowned in concentration, then opened her eyes wide.

"*Nooooh!*" She lunged toward the window but tripped over Irene's purse and crashed to the floor, smacking the side of her face on a corner of her desk as she fell.

"The b . . ." Molly raised herself only as far as her knees, one hand covering her right eye, her feet hopelessly tangled in the straps of Irene's bag. She flopped back down on the floor and crawled frantically to the window on her belly, propelling herself forward with one elbow and her knees.

"The bu . . ." Molly pulled herself up to the windowsill and peeked out over the street below, her one visible eye blazing with panic.

"The bus is at the corner!" she shrieked.

"We'd better hurry, girls, if we're going to get to school on time," Irene said, and headed for the door, seemingly unaware of the fact that Molly was now lying flat on her back, her legs kicking wildly, the bag binding her feet more tightly together with every move.

"Come on, princess, we'll grab an ice pack for that eye on the way to the bus stop," Irene called back to Molly. "Be a love, will you, and bring my purse."

Irene and the Marys hurried downstairs in a cheerful group as Molly struggled to jerk her feet from Irene's bag.

"I knew," Molly said grimly to the empty room, "that I was doomed without my notebook."

Chapter Two

Chance favors the prepared mind.

—*Molly's notebook*

"I don't know why you're so bent out of shape, Molly," Mary Margaret told her as they stood in front of their lockers before homeroom. Irene had deserted them immediately upon arrival at school, heading to the principal's office with a determined glint in her eye.

"I think Mrs. Flynn was right—it *was* a good idea for everyone on the bus to introduce themselves and share their special talent. I mean, my goodness, we've been going to school together forever and yet I never knew that Tommy Sullivan could sing.

Mrs. Flynn was smart to remember that getting-to-know-you exercise from her group tour to Vegas."

The other Marys nodded and Mary Pat turned to Mary Bridget.

"And I wouldn't have guessed that you could play your cello on a moving bus, Bridge. I'll be sure to tell your mom how good your arpeggios sounded this morning. You've been practicing."

Mary Bridget beamed and patted her cello case gently.

"Would you really, Pats? She's been furious with me since I left my cello on the bus again last week. She made me take a blood oath that I wouldn't set it down in public again. Which reminds me, Mol . . . after my orchestra practice this afternoon, could you take my cello home with you? I'll pick it up after dance class tonight."

Molly was on her hands and knees in front of her locker, squinting at a pile of textbooks. Her black eye had swollen shut and she had to twist her head to the left to focus on anything. It gave her a leering look.

"Sure, Mary Bridget. I've only got my grand-mother and her big black bag to deal with today.

What's a cello? But you owe me. So don't encourage Irene today. You three just egg her on. Remember my birthday party at the skating rink? You convinced her that she could flip and land that triple-jump thingie, never mind that she'd never skated before. And what happened? A broken elbow and six months of skating lessons, that's what."

"But it wasn't a compound fracture and you regained full range of motion in that arm, Mol. And your grandma only took the lessons because she felt so bad for crashing into you that way," Mary Margaret reminded her.

"Plus, I really enjoyed watching her compete that year. And I agree wholeheartedly with Mrs. Flynn: the judges *were* prejudiced against her because of her age. They should have let her advance to the regional finals because, after all, it wasn't her fault that her competitors were all only twelve years old."

The warning bell for homeroom rang before Molly could reply, and they joined the rush to be seated before the tardy bell rang two minutes later.

Because she could only see out of one eye and was handicapped by Irene's bag, which she pulled along the floor behind her, Molly careened into one person after another.

"Sorry . . . oops, excuse me . . . I apologize . . . my fault . . . I beg your pardon."

She finally arrived, breathless and a little bruised, in homeroom and collapsed gratefully at her desk.

She felt a surge of optimism. The worst, she thought, was probably over. She'd made it to school in, more or less, one piece. Granted, she didn't have her notebook, she *did* have Irene, and she now had a black eye and a heavy bag and, later in the day, a cello, too, but things were certain to quiet down.

"Attention!" The morning announcements began to boom through the school's public-address system. "Good morning, students of Our Lady of Mercy."

Molly sat attentively, listening to Monsignor Murphy, the principal.

"I'm delighted to share the news with you that we have a new student joining us today."

The hair on the back of Molly's neck slowly rose. She glanced around nervously and tried to shake the creepy feeling off.

19

"Our new student, as she prefers to be called"—Molly offered up a quick prayer to St. Jude, patron saint of lost causes—"and the sole guest of this year's Our Lady of Mercy Middle School Senior Citizens' Day, is Mrs. Irene Flynn, grandmother to our own Molly McGinty of the sixth grade."

The Marys let out whoops at Irene's and Molly's names. Molly slid down in her seat, willing herself to disappear. Her feeling of horror only intensified when she heard Jake Dempsey, *the* Jake Dempsey, wonder aloud, "Is that the lady in the purple pants?"

Molly stole a glance at the Marys. The mere sound of Jake's voice was enough to make them fall silent, if only temporarily. It was widely agreed upon by the girls of the sixth-grade class, more than a few seventh graders and a couple of eighth graders that Jake Dempsey was the best-looking boy they'd ever seen.

His name had been surreptitiously scribbled in many girls' notebooks—I ❤ Jake—since his family had moved into the neighborhood earlier that year.

The Marys diligently reported to Molly each and every encounter they had with Jake, as well as sharing information they'd gleaned about him. Jake was allergic to lemons, he loved gross-out comedy movies and in all likelihood he was going to be elected captain of the junior varsity football team next year.

Although she wouldn't admit it, even to the Marys, Molly also had a crush on him, but she was too shy to even speak to him.

Another reason to find her notebook quickly. What if Jake somehow discovered that she had opened a subfile on him? Nothing all that specific—for instance, she did not know his blood type yet, so the subfile was only half a page long and the information was, naturally, in code, so it wasn't likely that anyone would know what they were looking at should the notebook fall into the wrong hands, but Molly blushed to the roots of her hair at the thought of her Dempsey dossier.

Still, it wasn't as if she stalked him or anything.

Whenever they were in the same general vicinity, she dropped her gaze and stared fixedly at her notebook. Which was not to say that she didn't follow his every move when she was convinced he wouldn't notice her.

She was in agony whenever he sat next to Elaine Puckett at lunch and she'd silently cheered when he'd wound up in her homeroom, study period and shop class.

Molly waited patiently for the right time to speak with him. After all, she wanted to make the right impression. Or at least some impression. Right now he didn't really know she was alive. Yet admitting to the fact that the senior citizen with the questionable taste in clothes was her grandmother wasn't the sort of impression she'd had in mind.

Molly was saved from having to confess her relationship to Irene by the Marys.

"Mrs. Flynn is the greatest!" Mary Pat burbled to Jake.

"We're Molly's best friends in the whole world," Mary Bridget said, throwing an arm around Molly's shoulder and jerking her close.

"And we practically *live* at their house," Mary Margaret chimed in.

The other Marys nodded and jockeyed to get closer to Molly so that they could bask more directly in the reflected glory of Irene's appearance at school.

Molly stood, wishing she could think of something, anything, to say to Jake.

"Oh." He nodded and turned toward Molly. "That's cool that your grandmother came to school with you today, especially since no one else's grandparents ever come." He hesitated, peering at her. "You look different today."

Molly's mind scrambled between joy that Jake was finally talking to her and terror that he'd noticed her at all. She opened her mouth to speak.

"It's her black eye," Mary Bridget explained.

"She doesn't usually have one," Mary Pat pointed out.

"She fell down," Mary Margaret finished.

Jake continued to study Molly. "No, that's not it. I know! You don't have that binder you're always looking at."

Molly's heart, already racing just from the conversation, nearly burst. He noticed my notebook, she thought proudly. Any boy who appreciates the importance of a really well-organized notebook is even more perfect than I'd suspected.

"She lost it," Mary Margaret started.

"Yesterday," Mary Bridget continued.

"And it's a real tragedy, you know, because shekeepseverythinginthatnotebook," Mary Pat blurted out as she raced to finish her sentence before one of the other Marys interrupted her.

"Bummer." Jake looked as if he might say more, but the bell rang and he turned to grab his backpack.

Molly stood frozen as the surging Marys swept Jake from the room on a wave of chatter.

Well, that went well, Molly thought bitterly as she shuffled out of the room toward first period, dragging Irene's big black bag on the ground. It looked like roadkill.

Chapter Three

You get much better results if you use your skills and talents to work smoothly with those around you.

—*Molly's notebook*

"Where *is* she? I specifically told her not to be late to this class." Molly glanced nervously from the door to her watch. Her first-period French class was about to start. "I warned her that Sister Gloria hands out demerits for tardiness."

Molly and Mary Pat were sitting at their desks, motionless, with their eyes fixed straight ahead. They knew they risked being struck by a piece of chalk if Sister Gloria Gustavus caught them talking.

The girls had perfected an all but silent whisper and, as Mary Pat pointed out, Sister's aim wasn't what it used to be.

"Mrs. Flynn will show up, Molly," Mary Pat murmured. "The second bell hasn't rung yet."

"I don't know, Pats." Molly's lips barely moved. "I don't think Irene took me seriously when I told her how strict Sister Gloria is."

"You kind of have to experience Gloria Gustavus to believe her." Mary Pat spoke from behind a book she pretended to read. "My parents didn't believe she would give Chuckie Webber detention just because he had the hiccups."

"I've gotten perfect scores on all my tests in this class and I'm getting a C because I keep asking how to pronounce words," Molly said. "She thinks I'm challenging her authority when I ask questions."

Sister Gloria Gustavus spun around from the blackboard, where she had been writing conjugated verbs, and peered at her students over the tops of her glasses, ready to begin class the instant the second bell rang.

Irene floated through the door just as the bell

sounded. Molly gestured frantically at the empty seat between her and Mary Pat.

Instead, Irene took one look at Sister Gloria Gustavus and shrieked, "Gigi, my girl! How the *hell* are you?"

There was a moment of stunned silence. Sister Gloria gaped at Irene, who stood grinning in front of her.

"Don't just stand there—say something. It's been a long time since we were in a classroom together. What do you think of my new pants? Snazzy, huh? I'm here with my granddaughter. *Bonjour, chouchou.*" She blew a kiss at Molly, explaining to the class, "That's French for 'little cabbage.'"

Molly smiled weakly, wondering if she would fit under the desk, as Irene threw her arm around a still paralyzed Sister Gloria and glanced down at the teacher's desk. Irene picked up a book and paged through it.

"What *are* you teaching these poor souls?" she said with a snort.

She read from the book, translating into English, "'The cat sat on the chair. The dog is under the

27

table. The monkey sits on the branch.'" Irene rolled her eyes at the class.

"Are you kidding me? You'll never find a monkey in Paris, and none of this dog and cat stuff is going to come in handy at all."

The students stared at Irene adoringly—they'd wondered about the French animals too, and the knowledge that crusty Sister Gloria Gustavus was nicknamed Gigi was the most thrilling thing they'd learned in French class all year. The only one in the room not leaning forward to listen was Molly, who wondered if she had died and this was how it would be for all eternity, just constant embarrassment with Irene and no notebook and Jake wandering around thinking she was a geek. A one-eyed geek. A geek Cyclops. Quick, she thought, get control of your brain; you're going into shock.

Irene hopped up on the edge of Sister Gloria's desk and winked at the class.

"What you kids need is practical French. You know, phrases that you'll need to know when you go to France someday. Remember when we went to Paris, Gigi?" Irene threw back her head and laughed. Molly was shocked to see Sister Gloria blush. What had they done in Paris that would simultaneously delight Irene and embarrass Sister Gloria?

"Gigi and I went to the same high school and we traveled to Europe together after we graduated. I bet that waiter is still talking about us." Irene slapped her thigh. "I'm sure he'd never been arrested before."

"You got arrested, Mrs. Flynn?" Mary Pat asked.

"Only once. Nope, I take that back. We were also arrested in Amsterdam and, um . . . oh, yes, we were brought in for questioning by the captain of the ship we sailed on to Europe."

Molly glanced over at Sister Gloria, who had moved her chair to the front row of desks and was watching Irene as intently as anyone else in the room.

"So you see, *mes petites amours*, you'll need to know how to say to the police officers—that's *les gendarmes*—'What can I do for you, Officer?' and 'No, I don't know who threw that bottle,' and 'We did not run down the Champs Elysées naked.'"

Mary Pat finally broke the astonished silence. "Can you teach us how to swear in French?"

"Oh, sure, but frankly, if you réally want to swear in a foreign language, you just can't beat Italian for cursing. Or Spanish. Hemingway used to say that only the Spanish knew how to swear well. . . . I remember at a party once we were talking and he was a little bit drunk . . . Well, never mind that. It's just that Italian or Spanish is such a passionate way to express yourself."

Sister Gloria Gustavus cleared her throat softly and exchanged a glance with Irene.

"Well," Irene said, backpedaling, "maybe not actual swear words, and, since you are in French class, maybe we'd better concentrate on one language at a time. How about some perfectly nice French words that *sound* like swear words?"

"Let's get into small groups, *mes enfants*." Sister Gloria Gustavus leapt to her feet, bristling with energy. "We'll have adjectives that sound like swear words over here, verbs that sound insulting over there and nouns of a dubious nature in the front of the room."

Twenty-five pairs of eyes looked in amazement at the stranger Sister Gloria Gustavus had become. As if on a string, all their heads pivoted toward Irene, who had crossed her legs and was swinging a foot casually, a satisfied look in her eye.

"Chop-chop," Sister Gloria said. "There *will* be a test on this material later."

The class jumped out of their seats and quickly formed small groups.

"Poodle"—Irene motioned to Molly—"you take the verb group, okay? I'm sure you know tons of interesting-sounding action words."

As Molly slowly made her way across the room, her uniform got snagged on the broken crank of the window and as she jerked free, a big chunk of material was torn from the skirt.

"Oh, no," Molly sighed, trying to hold the tattered edges of her hem together.

"Too bad miniskirts aren't allowed in school, because you have very nice legs, dumpling," Irene commented.

"Almost as good as yours, Irene," Sister Gloria called out with what passed for a giggle. "Say, is that

Charlie Blake still after you the way he was in high school?"

Mary Pat nudged Molly. "I bet that's Mary Margaret's great-uncle Charlie! He's got a huge crush on Mrs. Flynn, you know." She nodded sagely.

Molly ignored Mary Pat as she pulled up a chair and opened her French book, searching for some interesting words that sounded bad.

Well, Molly thought, even if it's dirty, at least Irene has us studying French. Maybe things won't go so badly after all.

Chapter Four

Adequate preparation is vital to effectiveness.
—*Molly's notebook*

Molly looked up from her math test. Her eyes were burning and her neck was stiff. She'd been so engrossed in the math problems that she hadn't moved for the first thirty minutes of class. But she had answered all the questions and she felt good about her solutions, although she wasn't as confident as she would have been if she'd had her own notes to study from the night before.

She glanced around the room, trying to gauge the progress of her classmates. She was relieved to see Renee Potter scratching her elbow and Ryan

Deck tugging on his left earlobe. She knew then that the two top students in class were struggling too.

Irene had taught Molly how to play poker one rainy weekend, and although Molly didn't care for card games, she had been fascinated by Irene's explanation of what she called tells, nervous habits that gave you away when you were trying to bluff and appear calm. Molly had made a list of nervous habits in her now missing notebook.

Irene.

Molly's stomach clenched. Her grandmother had been entirely too quiet during the test, and a quiet Irene was a dangerous Irene.

Molly leaned over to whisper to Irene in the next row but was jerked backward in her seat by a sharp tug on her hair.

"Sit *still*," a voice hissed from behind, "I'm almost done."

Out of the corner of her eye, Molly tried to catch a glimpse of the person who was holding her hair, but when she moved her head even slightly her hair was quickly and viciously yanked. She sat, silent and still, trying to figure out what was happening to her head, and who was doing it. She saw Sister Catherine leave the room with the attendance sheet in hand.

"That's a cute look," Irene said as soon as the door closed behind Sister. "Did you ever think about adding some beads?"

"I'm a little short on supplies at the moment," a husky voice answered from behind Molly. "All I've got to work with are these tiny rubber bands from my braces."

"Very resourceful of you. How long does a hairdo like that last?" Molly sat stupefied, listening to her grandmother and her unseen, self-appointed hairdresser getting to know each other.

"Oh, weeks if you do a tight enough braid. My brother leaves his in for ages."

"I'm Irene. Could you do that to my hair during lunch? Here." Irene leaned into Molly's limited range of vision as she reached for an object on the floor near Molly's feet. "You dropped one."

"Thanks. These suckers boing all over if you're not careful, and my orthodontist has started charging me for replacement packets, so I've only got access to a limited supply each month. There." The owner of the voice poked Molly in the shoulder. "You can move now."

Molly turned to see a girl with rhinestone-trimmed cat-eye glasses and a small hot pink and orange boa tied around her neck, cracking her knuckles contentedly. This girl had transferred to Our Lady of Mercy from the public middle school on the other side of town the week before.

"What did you do to me?" Molly demanded. She reached up and felt a scattering of little braids on the left side of the back of her head.

The rogue hairdresser ignored her question and turned to Irene.

"Nice to meet you, Irene. My name is Brenda, but I wish it was Benet because that sounds more glamorous, and I can do your hair at lunch if you eat during fifth period."

"Do we, pumpkin?" Irene asked Molly, who was lightly fingering the tiny, tight braids covering the back of her head, a horrified look on her face.

"Why," Molly wailed, "did you Rasta-braid my hair?"

"They're not Rasta braids, sweetheart," Irene explained. "Because then your hair would just kind of hang in clumpy bits. These are more like cornrows, because they're tiny, but very distinct, braids."

"Uh-huh," Molly responded to her grandmother in a cold, flat tone before turning to Brenda/Benet. "Regardless of what they *are*, why did you *do* them to me? I don't even know you."

"Doing your hair seemed like a good way to break the ice, since we've never actually spoken before now and I didn't have to take the test because I just moved here. Besides, you looked like you needed to have some fun with your look," Brenda/Benet answered, handing Molly a mirrored compact.

"That's *exactly* what I said to her this morning!" Irene gloated as Molly stared wide-eyed at her reflection.

"You'd be a great client," Brenda/Benet said, smiling at Molly. "You never even noticed me while you were taking your test. Plus, I thought doing this to your hair would make you look more like your grandma. I noticed right off when you walked in together that she's got a real zippy look going for her."

"How'd you learn how to do hair like that, Benet?" Irene asked.

"I taught myself after I couldn't find anyone to do my hair the way I like it."

"Oh, honey, I *know*. Trying to find a good hairdresser is as annoying as that television commercial about feminine itch—"

"That's not really the point, Irene," Molly interrupted as she continued to gaze doubtfully at the mirror.

"So," Irene continued, "you girls sit next to each other in math class and you don't even know each other? That's a shame. School is all about making friends, you know. I can honestly say that no one has asked me what the capital of Rhode Island is since I was in second grade. And learning long division was a total waste of time, seeing as calculators do all that borrowing and carrying and whatnot so effectively."

"Binder Girl up there doesn't seem to notice anything that's not in that notebook of hers," Brenda/Benet commented, a bit acidly, Molly felt. "I figured that I needed a unique way to introduce myself to her. You've got to take the initiative, my dad says, when you're the new girl."

"I don't know how she could have missed you, Benet. Is that a safety pin in your ear?"

"Kilt pin."

"I do love a girl with a strong sense of personal style. Especially since you have to wear these drab school uniforms. Navy blue is not," Irene confided, "a color that does anyone a favor, if you know what I mean."

"That's why I wear lingerie that I buy at Herb's House of the Second Time Around Clothing Store."

Despite herself, Molly found that she was becoming interested in the conversation.

"How kicky!" Irene cooed.

"Wanna see?" Brenda/Benet took a furtive look toward the door to make sure Sister Catherine was not about to reenter the room. Then she lifted her skirt a few inches to show the hem of a pair of lime green tap pants over her striped tights. Molly noticed a number of male heads turning quickly. It was amazing—they must have heard the sound of fabric sliding. Like bats hearing flies' wings.

39

"I'm not really into school." Brenda/Benet dropped her skirt. "But I love fashion. I'm going to be a stylist when I grow up."

"A girl after my own heart."

"Would you like to see my portfolio?" Brenda/Benet dug a three-ring binder out of her backpack. Molly whimpered softly at the sight of the binder. Despite her lack of interest in fashion, she was drawn to anyone who organized their life in a binder.

Brenda/Benet dropped the portfolio on her desk with a thunk. Molly nearly salivated at the sight of the table of contents.

"See, I've broken it down into different topics. I've even redesigned some baseball teams' uniforms."

"Baseball?" Irene's face lit up at the mention of one of her obsessions.

"Different topics?" Molly repeated, beaming.

"Yup. See, most people think stylists just help supermodels pick out boots and bikinis. But I have bigger plans. I want to completely reshape the face of style and design in America. I have ideas on everything. Baby clothes, armchairs, airport restrooms, the Pentagon—I've got plans to make *everything* more visually appealing."

Molly and Irene flipped through the portfolio, Irene complimenting Brenda/Benet on her bold use of leopard skin and chintz throw pillows in taxis and Molly grinding her teeth at the sight of a notebook that surpassed her own in terms of subfiles.

"Do you really like my work?" Brenda/Benet chewed briefly on a fingernail before pulling her hand away from her mouth. "I shouldn't bite my nails when I get nervous. It's a bad habit."

"There's nothing wrong with bad habits," Irene told her. "Where would we be without our bad habits? They're what separates us from the dreary souls amongst us."

"I thought you said the ability to accessorize was what separated us from the dreary souls amongst us," Mary Pat said.

Molly looked up, startled. She saw that the entire class had gathered around their desks. Most of the girls were poring over Brenda/Benet's portfolio, most of the boys were gawking at Brenda/Benet, and Chipper Lopez was admiring Molly's new hairdo.

"Well, that, too," Irene told her. "The only exceptions to those rules are animals. Animals," Irene added, nodding, "are the perfect people."

"That's what I think too," Brenda/Benet said. "The only thing wrong with them is that, except for the simian family and cats, they don't self-groom."

Molly looked up with approving eyes from Brenda/Benet's impressively configured portfolio. Well, she thought, she may be as flaky as Irene, but at least she appreciates the importance of structure.

Chapter Five

A to-do list helps set priorities and focuses on important tasks.

—*Molly's notebook*

Molly and Mary Margaret huddled together at a table in the corner of the library during their study period. Molly had ditched Irene after math, sending her, with a sigh of relief, to the teachers' lounge.

Third period was the highlight of both Mary Margaret's and Molly's day. Mary Margaret looked forward to an entire hour of gazing at Jake, and Molly spent the hour sprucing up her notebook. Although she stole peeks at Jake, she prided herself on the discipline she showed in refraining from watching him except during those brief peek breaks every seven minutes.

Since Molly now feared that her notebook was lost forever, she was concentrating on cobbling together a replacement. She felt better immediately once she had a to-do list in front of her again.

"Oh, look." Mary Margaret poked Molly's arm. "Outside."

Molly looked through the window and saw Irene holding the hands of two small kindergarteners from the school next door, who were leading her along the sidewalk with the rest of their class. Irene waved merrily and pointed out Molly and Mary Margaret to her new friends. Thirty tiny faces turned to face them and, at a sign from Irene, thirty kindergarteners made a perfectly synchronized bow in Molly's direction.

Molly cringed and buried her head in her notebook.

"Nuts," she whispered to Mary Margaret. "Irene will probably bring home a plaster of Paris handprint or a papier-mâché globe."

"I don't know why you're so hard on Mrs. Flynn, Molly. She's a hoot."

"You wouldn't think she was so great, Mags, if she was your grandmother."

"Yes, I would. One of my grandmothers keeps calling me Jeffrey. She gets me confused with my brother. And my other grandmother makes me call her Mrs. Blake—she says being called Grandmother will ruin her golf game. I love Mrs. Flynn—she's the most fun ever."

"You only think she's so wonderful because she won that bet with your dad and made him raise your allowance. I feel sorry for him—who knew she could arm wrestle like that?"

"What's so awful about having a fun grandma?"

"She's . . . well, she's impossible to live with, that's what. For instance, she talks to everyone— do you know who came to dinner last Sunday? Father James, State Representative Wolfe and some guy who makes dirty movies. Nobody ate a thing. Everyone screamed and hollered about morality, the First Amendment and profit margins all night."

"Dirty movies? Really? How'd she meet him?" Mary Margaret's eyes were huge with awe.

"She says she meets lots of interesting people in her business. And that's another thing, that crazy job of hers. Do you know what she did last week? Called all around town trying to find an animal psychiatrist. And do you know why? Because Clover the racing turtle was depressed."

"Oh, that's too bad. How's he feeling now?"

"Mary Margaret, it's a turtle. Turtles don't get depressed. They don't race, either."

"Mrs. Flynn must have had a good reason for thinking Clover was sad."

"Yeah, something about losing his competitive edge. Irene claims she could tell that Clover deliberately threw his last race at the county fair two weeks ago."

"Well, she would know, Mol. I mean, she *is* a professional. She told me she's got the largest agency in this part of the country."

"That's because no one in their right mind is a talent representative for animals."

"They're more than animals, Molly, they're clients."

"What's the difference?"

"A fifteen-percent commission."

"Geez, Mags, you're even starting to sound like her."

"Thanks. Mrs. Flynn is the most interesting person I've ever known."

"She told me once that she used to be afraid that nothing interesting would ever happen to her," Molly said. "I'm afraid interesting things will never *stop* happening to her." She paused, looking miserable. "I just want things to be quiet and normal and organized. Do you remember when she insisted that we eat organic vegetarian food, when we were being friends of the environment? And then she didn't have time to get to the health-food store? All we had to eat for a week was free-range soy or whatever that lumpy white stuff was, and the squash your mother sent over from her garden."

"I'd never eaten soy enchiladas before, much less squash pâté, and those soy-squash sloppy joes were wild," Mary Margaret said. "But that's what makes her so neat. My great-uncle Charlie says Mrs. Flynn has moxie."

"I don't even know what moxie is."

"A plucky attitude, a good sense of humor and a great ra— Well, never mind, that's just what Great-uncle Charlie says."

"And that's all well and good, but everything about Irene is always so . . . disorganized. I hate that, Mary Margaret. I really do. Irene is so dramatic and unpredictable."

At that very instant, the other Marys burst into the library and in one voice screeched, "Molly, your grandmother just got busted for smoking in the girls' bathroom!"

Chapter Six

Respond swiftly and calmly to new developments.
—*Molly's notebook*

"Lamb, what happened to you?" Irene looked up from the bench outside the principal's office to see Molly standing in the doorway, seething and dripping ink on the floor.

"Michael Parady was so excited to hear that you'd gotten in trouble that he accidentally dumped a bottle of ink on me. I warned him about that silly fountain pen, but oh, no, he *had* to bring it to the library."

"He's a sweet boy. But why are you here? Don't you have class?"

"Irene." Molly looked around. The Trouble Bench, as it was popularly known, was actually two benches full of students waiting to be talked to by Monsignor Murphy, and Irene was sitting contentedly, surrounded by what Molly had always regarded as the dregs of the entire school. "The Marys told me—actually, they told the entire library and most of the third floor—that you had been sent to the principal's office for smoking. What were you thinking?"

"The kindergarteners had snack time, and since I don't like graham crackers, I wandered over to the teachers' lounge. But I got very bored there—everyone was so quiet and the coffee was terrible. So then I went for a walk and ran into Carly here." Irene draped a chummy arm around the girl sitting next to her, who glared sullenly at Molly.

"She was on her way to the ladies' room," Irene continued, "so I thought I'd go with her and powder my nose. Erica and Chloe"—she nodded toward two terrifying-looking girls who were picking black polish off their fingernails—"were smoking in one of the stalls when we arrived."

"Fine. So why are you and, uh, Carly here if you were just powdering your nose?"

"As much as I personally disapprove of smoking, I didn't understand why that hall monitor creature had to be so nasty to the girls. She walked in, caught them and proceeded to give them de-whatsit."

"Detention."

"Yes, detention. Well, I don't know what that is, but it sounded bad, dear. I wouldn't have been so upset had I not, with my very eyes, seen that—what did you call her, Erica? hall Nazi?—smoking in the teachers' lounge just moments before. It was the hypocrisy more than the punishment against which I had to take a stand."

"Yeah. Freaking authority figures think they can boss us around," Chloe snarled. Erica raised a clenched fist in a gesture of solidarity as Irene and Carly high-fived.

"So then what happened? How did you wind up here?"

"Mrs. Flynn was awesome." Erica jumped to her feet. "She tried to get us off the hook, but the hall monster told her to mind her own business."

"Yeah, and then the hall witch grabbed our arms and started to pull us into the hall with her," Chloe added.

"Then Mrs. Flynn told the hall hag to remove her hands from them," Carly explained, "and I thought she wanted me to take a swing at the old bat, so I did."

"You hit the hall monitor?" Molly turned to Irene. "You didn't *want* her to hit the hall monitor, did you?"

"No, of course not. Violence is never the solution. But"—Irene turned and hastened to reassure Carly—"I can see where you might have gotten that idea. My voice *was* very firm." She turned back to Molly. "And, to be fair, Carly didn't actually strike her."

"So now what happens?" Molly asked.

"I'm sure we'll get things cleared up with the monsignor—just as soon as he's able to see us. There's quite a line today." Irene didn't look at all disappointed by the idea of spending an entire class period visiting with the Detention Squad.

"Take a seat, pussycat. You're dripping ink all over the floor," Irene said offhandedly to Molly. Her attention had been captured by a covert poker game that had started in the corner of the room.

Molly sighed in resignation before she squeezed onto a bench—the kids on it seemed quite willing to give her room once they saw her eye, the dead bag she was dragging and the trail of ink she was leaving behind—and gingerly opened her science book, careful not to leave inky fingerprints.

She'd get notes from Mary Pat later. If she read the next chapter on her own, she wouldn't fall behind just because she had to miss class to help Irene plead for the elimination of hypocrisy in middle school disciplinary policies. Molly was quickly lost in a history of germ theory, tuning out the commotion surrounding her.

"Uh, excuse me, but you seem to be on fire."

Molly's head jerked up and she looked into the face of Tommy Adams, the scariest boy at Our Lady of Mercy Middle School. Molly had been warned by the Marys to steer clear of Tommy and his bunch. They were responsible, it was rumored, for the mysteriously dwindling squirrel population in the neighborhood. Molly remembered jotting a reminder in her notebook to follow up on the plans she'd heard that Tommy was making to actually build the perfect mousetrap once his experiments with the local rodents were complete.

Mary Pat's older brother, Clinton, was in Tommy's Screaming Madness rock band. After they practiced in Tommy's father's garage, Clinton was left temporarily deafened and walked around screaming "What did you say?" for several hours.

Tommy reached over and brushed at Molly's shoulder.

"There. You weren't actually on fire. Just slightly singed from a couple of pieces of burning paper that landed on you. Must have been those guys." He jerked his head at three boys who were giggling maniacally and tossing lit matches at each other now that the drama of Molly in flames had ended without serious casualties.

Molly frantically twisted around on the bench, trying in vain to look at her own back and reassure herself that she wasn't still smoldering.

She finally found her voice and stammered a trembling "Th-thanks."

"Hey, great shiner. You've gotta be pretty tough if you can take a smack like that," Tommy told her with an admiring glance.

Molly reached up to touch her face, caught sight of her blue-black hands and tucked them quickly under the now jagged hem of her skirt. "Oh . . . uh . . . well . . . not exactly."

"Who's the old lady in the wild pants?"

"My grandmother."

"What did they get you for?"

"I beg your pardon?"

Tommy spoke slowly, as if to a dim-witted child. "Why . . . are . . . you . . . in . . . the . . . principal's . . . office?"

"Oh, um, well, you see . . ."

"I only asked because if your grandma had to come down to bail you out, it must have been a beaut."

"I got busted for smoking in the girls' room," Irene called out proudly. "I'm a juvenile delinquent. She's just here for support." She beamed fondly at Molly.

"Cool." Tommy looked impressed.

Molly shifted awkwardly on the hard bench, reluctant to get lost in her reading again. The firebugs might try to incinerate her once more if they noticed that her attention had wandered.

"So." She cleared her throat. "What did *you* do?"

"I beat the snot out of Todd."

"I don't know any To—wait a minute, you mean Todd the fifth grader in Advanced Placement classes? You beat the snot out of *that* Todd?"

"He's got a real attitude. I didn't appreciate his tone."

"But he's, like, well, only ten, isn't he?"

"Ten and a half. Look, he's my cousin, okay? And I didn't really beat him up; I just stuffed him in a locker. Would have worked, too." Tommy gazed off into the distance for a moment. "But I underestimated how loud the little booger can scream. So," he said, abruptly changing the subject. "Why are *you* here to plead Granny Rebel's case, instead of your folks?"

Molly took a shaky breath. Irene looked over sharply and opened her mouth to speak, just as Tommy sympathetically patted Molly's shoulder and Molly, studying her ink-splotched fingers, answered quietly.

"My folks died in a car accident when I was little and Irene . . . well, she wanted me." She raised her head and met Irene's eyes, which had been fixed on her during this explanation. Irene nodded and turned back to her conversation with Carly.

"Trust me, it's almost worth it to be an orphan to live with such a great old lady," Tommy told Molly.

"You think so?"

"Yeah, sure. My folks are drunks. Mean drunks, if you want the full story. They scream a lot."

"Irene never screams. She took singing lessons once and she chanted for a while during her yoga phase, neither of which sounded very good, but no screaming. Oh, wait, she did a thing called primal screaming once, a kind of vocal thing to help meditation, but she had to stop because all the cats in the neighborhood kept coming to sing to her and kept the neighbors awake all night."

"Say," Irene called out to the entire population of the Trouble Bench, "when we're done speaking with Monsignor Murphy, let's all get together and do lunch."

"Your grandma rocks," Tommy told Molly as they watched Irene scowl at the handheld video game someone handed her. It was her turn to set the new world record for roasting aliens from the planet Zarduck.

Chapter Seven

Achievement, success and high levels of
effectiveness are not determined by your genes.
—*Molly's notebook*

"That went well," Irene announced as she, Molly
and the Marys arrived in the lunchroom, a band of
Irene's new friends from the principal's office
trailing behind them. "I must say, Monsignor
Murphy is a very understanding man."

"I don't think our meeting went well at all, Irene,"
Molly said. "My name got added to the detention list
because I cut class to help defend you. In a room
full of future felons, petty thieves and maybe one

potential serial killer, I'm the only one who's going to wind up actually being punished."

"That's certainly an ironic twist, isn't it, cupcake?" Irene patted Molly's shoulder. "Maybe I should have a talk with that science teacher of yours. I seem to have a knack for this kind of thing. And besides, it's not fair that you should be punished."

"No! I'll fix it myself. The last thing Our Lady of Mercy needs today is another debate about the nature of injustice from Irene Flynn."

"You shouldn't be so quick to reject my help, baby. Didn't you see me impress the monsignor with my quick thinking?"

"Irene, he was so confused and frightened by your claims of abuse of power and authoritarian brutality that he'd have said anything to get you and all your new buddies out of his office."

"Well, peaches, you know what they say: If you can't dazzle 'em with your brilliance, then baffle 'em with your bulls—"

"You'll probably drive the poor man to an early grave, Irene."

Molly had been so busy squabbling with Irene

that she hadn't noticed they were now sitting in the section of the lunchroom that boasted the highest crime rate in the school. Molly looked up just in time to see Irene deftly catch a carton of milk that had been hurled in their general direction.

Molly recognized most of the kids she and Irene had just met from the Trouble Bench, as well as a few who were so intimidating that they flew well under the radar of disciplinary detection at Our Lady of Mercy. They hung out after hours with the high school students from across the street and couldn't be bothered with middle school mischief. Taking over small countries would be more their style, Molly thought.

Molly and the Marys always sat on the other side of the cafeteria, where they studied, talked quietly and kept a wary eye on this side of the room.

Two of the Marys were now clutching their lunch boxes to their chests, looking around them in awe. Mary Bridget, whom Molly had always considered the boldest of the group, was tentatively offering to share a plastic Baggie of carrots with an eighth grader who was busily applying more black eyeliner. Judging from the way she would study Molly and then gaze into her small mirror while dabbing at her own eye with the makeup, Mary Bridget's lunch companion was trying to duplicate Molly's black-eyed look.

Molly sighed and had started to rise and head for the lunch line before she realized that her lunch tickets were in her lost notebook.

"Oh, Irene, I don't have lunch tickets for us."

"Don't worry, pooky, lunch is on me. Now," Irene said as she looked around the cafeteria expectantly, "just who do I speak to about payment? Give me my purse and let me get my credit card."

"This is a school lunchroom. They don't take plastic."

"Too bad. I wanted to try that interesting-looking tuna thing. Well, give me my purse anyway. I'm sure I have something to nibble on."

A chorus of voices piped up with offers to share lunch, and a grubby-looking boy thrust an equally shabby roast beef sandwich at Irene.

"Here, Mrs. Flynn, you can have half of my lunch."

"Thanks, hon, but I never eat anything I could possibly represent, and Sparky the cow is a particular favorite of mine. You're sweet to worry, but we'll make do with whatever I can find in my purse."

She dug through her bag, setting various items on the table as she searched.

She pulled out a small squeaky toy in the shape of a pork chop. "We were trying to get Fluffy the rottweiler to look at the camera for his head shot— he's going to be the face on all the billboards for Billy Ray's Security World," she explained proudly.

She then yanked a trailing piece of white tulle from her bag. "Now, why would I have a bridal veil in my bag? You don't suppose," she joked, elbowing Mary Margaret in the ribs, "that I was going to elope this weekend, do you? Ah, well . . ." She shrugged happily.

A wrinkled but unused airsickness bag was the next item she set on the table. "Some of my clients get an attack of nerves before their close-ups. Although," she said, pondering, "I've never actually gotten a cat to yack in a barf bag—yet. But we dwell in possibility."

Irene hummed softly as she continued to sort through her purse. Everyone at the table was now leaning toward her, waiting to see what she would pull from the bag next. Molly rubbed her shoulder, wondering how much damage carrying the bulky purse had done to her muscles, joints and tendons. She felt . . . what? Old. She felt old. And Irene looked younger all the time. It's the bag that does it, Molly thought. Carrying the bag is aging me before my time. She shook her head. I'm getting old and I'm going insane.

"Oh, good!" Irene exclaimed. "The sonnets of Shakespeare. I've been meaning to memorize these for ages, and I'm always afraid I'll get stuck on a bus with nothing to read.

"Look, jewel! I found the remote control to the television set. I remember now—I tucked it in my handbag to remind me to watch that special on Komodo dragons. Did you know they'll bite a goat and then track it for days, waiting for it to die from the infection so they can eat it? There's something to be said for that kind of patience." Irene tossed the remote back into the bag and continued her search for something edible.

"You should go on that television game show where you win prizes for having the most unusual things—I bet you'd win a bundle, Mrs. Flynn," Mary Margaret said.

"I think you're right, Mary Bridget."

"Mary Margaret."

"Whatever." From the depths of the purse, Irene finally pulled a crumpled brown paper bag. "Here we go, my very favorite food group: chocolate-covered coffee beans!"

She plunged her hand into the paper bag and popped a few beans into her mouth, munching happily as Brenda/Benet, who had been hovering nearby since the beginning of the lunch period, began to braid her hair.

"Lovey, don't you want to get the other side of your hair braided?" Irene asked Molly.

"No," Molly said as she reached for a handful of coffee beans. "I can't wait to get this side unbraided. I'm not about to have my entire head done."

"Well, there's a pleasing symmetry to having a black eye on the right and cornrows on the left."

"We have to have broccoli for dinner tonight, Irene, for the antioxidants to cleanse all this chocolate and caffeine from our systems. This is not a good lunch—

we're not getting our daily recommended amount of anything."

"I know," Irene said, tossing a few more beans into her mouth. "Isn't it almost too good to be true?"

Molly shook her head sadly and looked over at the Marys, who were peering at a boy who had lifted his shirt up to give them a detailed explanation of the homemade tattoo on his stomach. Mary Bridget reached out to trace the pattern with her finger.

"It's not really a tattoo," the boy said. "Not yet, I mean. I just used a ballpoint pen and a pocketknife for some of it. BoBo from Tattoo Heaven won't touch you if you're under eighteen. Something to do with his parole agreement. But as soon as I'm old enough, I'm gonna get one."

Molly had been absentmindedly eating chocolate-covered coffee beans as she observed the scene around her. She didn't realize that the caffeine was starting to make her jittery until Tommy Adams pulled out the chair next to her and she nearly jumped out of her skin. Her sudden gesture startled Tommy, and his cafeteria tray tipped. It seemed to happen in slow motion. The whole plate of spaghetti slid off his tray and hit Molly square in the chest.

"Dear heart," Irene called to Molly, ignoring the fact that Molly was now covered in pasta and tomato sauce. "Kyle here is coming to work for us. He's going to help out with Mick."

The Marys rushed over to Molly with paper napkins and tried to wipe Tommy's lunch off her. Molly glared at them and snatched the napkins away, swiping furiously at her blouse and then turning to Irene, who was deep in conversation with the boy who'd tried to share his sandwich with her earlier.

"Mickey the monkey who eats his own—"

"Yup, that's the one," Irene interrupted, and shot Molly a fierce look before turning back to Kyle with a too-bright smile. "I bet that when you woke up this morning, you had no idea you'd be a monkey wrangler by lunchtime, did you?"

Kyle flushed with pride. He said to the rest of the lunch table, "Mickey is famous, you know, a real celebrity. He's the mascot on the Big Jack's House of Used Cars commercials, and I'm going to look after him on the days he's working."

"You know"—Irene looked thoughtful—"now

that I think about it, there are any number of jobs around my agency. Anyone else looking for a little pocket money?"

The entire table erupted, grabbing for the business cards Irene was handing out.

"Oh, great," Molly said to the Marys. "Now all these freakazoids are going to be hanging around. It was bad enough when Cricket the magic-trick cat went into labor and Irene was afraid to leave her on her own. You remember. She not only brought the cat home, but she also invited Grant the magician, his assistant Miss Dixie, the breeder, Dr. Emma and her two veterinary students, Mary Margaret's great-uncle Charlie and the guy who reroofed our house, to watch. They stayed with us for days waiting for that cat to have kittens."

"We were kitty midwives, Molly, and, don't forget, that was a high-risk pregnancy," Mary Pat said. "We witnessed the miracle of birth on your bed."

"No, Mary Pat, what we witnessed was the creation of a stain that I can't get out of my pillow." Molly looked around glumly. "But at least that was a one-time deal. You just know Irene's going to encourage everyone to drag all those ugly beasts back to our house so she can teach them about the business."

"Oh, Molly . . ." The voices of three horrified Marys chimed in. "You don't mean that. Not 'ugly beasts.'"

"Okay," Molly said grumpily. "The animals aren't all hideous, and I really like Claude the chameleon. But Irene will probably try to adopt a few of her new employees."

"That's not an altogether bad thing, Mol. Look." Mary Pat nudged her.

Molly looked across the table and felt her heart pound suddenly. There sat Jake Dempsey with one of Irene's business cards in his hand.

"Oh, well, then," Molly said. "Maybe it won't be so horrible if Irene hires *some* people from school to work for her."

Chapter Eight

The simple process of coordinating the actions of a group of people can instantly accelerate their effectiveness.

—*Molly's notebook*

"Molly, great news! We have a sub in English today," Mary Bridget said, greeting her when she arrived in class with Irene. "And that's not the best part."

"Mrs. Meyers?" Molly guessed.

"Yeah. How great is that? I bet you five dollars she doesn't even notice that Mrs. Flynn is old. No offense, Mrs. Flynn."

"None taken, Mary Margaret."

"Mary Bridget."

"Whatever."

Molly pushed Irene toward an empty seat in her row. Irene looked at Mrs. Meyers with a calculating eye.

"So," she said to Molly, "tell me about this substitute teacher."

"She's a ditz," Mary Bridget said. "Whenever she fills in for any of our classes we have sustained silent reading time because by the time she figures out the lesson plan, the class period is over."

"That's a huge waste of your valuable time," Irene said. "Not the reading part, of course, which is always worthwhile, nor do I object to the fact that she deviates from the expected. But part of the reason you go to school is to share ideas with each other."

"I thought you said that part of the reason we went to school is to fulfill the deal we have with society," Mary Bridget said to Irene. "You know, the deal you were telling us about in which we work hard to grow up and cease to be pesky little kids anymore and if we're lucky we later get to pay income tax for that privilege."

"That, too," Irene answered, then began ticking reasons off on her fingers. "One, you go to school to make friends—I've said that many times. Two, you go to learn how to become not pesky—once you're educated, it's called inquisitive. And three, you go to share ideas—which may well be the most important aspect of all. To ignore a perfectly good opportunity for discussion and debate is nothing short of criminal." By the time she'd finished speaking, Irene's eyes were shining.

"Everyone likes quiet reading time," Molly said hopefully. Uh-oh. Irene was sizing up the room.

Irene jumped to her feet and marched to the front of the class with a determined air.

She greeted Mrs. Meyers breezily. "Hello. I'm Irene Flynn, and with your permission, I'd like to teach this class today. Just until you straighten out the lesson plan, of course."

"That would be very helpful." Mrs. Meyers smiled up at her dimly. As Mary Bridget had predicted, Mrs. Meyers gave no indication that she found Irene's age or her request at all out of the ordinary. "I'll just try to figure out what we're supposed to be doing this afternoon. I never can read the notes they leave me."

"All right, then." Irene rubbed her hands together as she faced the classroom. "What should we talk about today? What class is this, anyway? Not that it matters—we can chat about anything."

"This is English class," Molly called out, "and we're reading—"

"We'll have a poetry slam," Irene interrupted. "They're all the rage.

"We take turns standing up for thirty seconds at a time to recite original poetry," she explained to the sea of blank faces. "Obviously, since no one knew this was going to happen and we are not, therefore, prepared, we'll be spontaneous. Just create a poem about anything that comes to mind."

No one moved. There was a kind of stunned silence. Right, Molly thought, they'll do poetry. Right. Out of nowhere they'll do poetry. She propped her elbow on her desk and rested her head on her hand, waiting.

"You have to think of poetry," Irene continued after a moment, "as a form of jazz or the blues—

a kind of performance art. You improvise and you express yourself. You don't have to worry about being good. They don't have to rhyme. Just be honest. You can talk about anything that interests you, just as long as there is the free exchange of ideas amongst peers."

Kyle from lunch stood up. "I have an honest poem that expresses my own self."

"Excellent. Let's hear what you have to say," Irene said.

Kyle walked to the front of the room and cleared his throat. "Ahem." He stood tall and rolled his head a few times to work the kinks out of his neck. He clasped his hands behind his back, carefully aligned his toes on a crack in the floor and took a deep breath.

"My own dog. Pizza for breakfast. A cherry fifty-seven Chevy when I turn sixteen. This is all I want in life. A poem by Kyle Bendecker."

He bowed as the class applauded. Irene patted him on the back as he made his way to his seat. Mary Bridget immediately jumped to her feet and headed for the front of the room.

"The hours of practice, full of mistakes, wet with tears. Endless scales and impossible phrases. All worth it for the one time I play Beethoven as he meant it. So what if I'm the only one who ever hears it. A poem by Mary Bridget Sheehan." Mary Bridget blushed and curtsied, then hurried back to her seat. The class whooped and cheered as she threw an arm around the cello case that was propped against her desk.

Mrs. Meyers surprised everyone by suddenly standing.

"Blue ribbons. Red, ripe tomatoes. Glittering trophies. Golden apple pies. Medals to hang from my neck. Marge Sinclair pea green with envy. The perfect county fair. A poem by Lucy Meyers."

She nodded happily and sat down again. Irene flashed her a thumbs-up.

The ringing of a phone interrupted the slam. Irene unclipped the cell phone from her belt. "*Buon giorno*, Val, what's going on?"

"Valerie is her executive assistant," Mary Bridget explained to the class. "Mrs. Flynn says she sets the standard for excellence in the field of quality office management."

"She did what? How large is the crowd now? Talk to me, Val. I can't help you if you don't stop crying. . . . Uh-huh. . . . Stay with me, now—is anyone actually dead? What happened then? Well, that's not so bad. . . . Is she still missing? . . . I'm sure that's covered by insurance. . . . Not if the snake hadn't been fed recently, you say. Hmmm, remind me to upgrade that policy."

"Do you think she's talking about Rhonda the anaconda, Mol?" Mary Bridget looked worried.

Molly held her head in her hands and answered wearily, "I think so, but I'd probably know for sure, Bridge, if I had my notebook. I always keep a copy of Irene's clients' schedules in case I need to get in touch with her when she's on location." Under her breath, she added, "And I *know* I had a copy of that insurance rider she's talking about."

"Well, there's nothing much to do right now except to cancel my scuba lesson and set up a meeting with Vinnie first thing Monday morning. . . . Vinnie my lawyer, not Vinnie my dance instructor. . . . No, they're not the same person. . . . Yes, I'm sure. . . . Because I've had dinner with both of them and my lawyer doesn't cha-cha very well."

Irene looked up at the class and tapped the fingers of one hand together to indicate that Val was yammering on and on. Everybody nodded in sympathy.

"As long as I've got you on the phone, Valerie, give me a rundown of today's phone messages. . . . Uh-huh. . . . Call Judge Morgan back and tell her that of course she can borrow my bike, but remind Her Honor that she hasn't returned my tent yet. . . . Sammy the potbellied pig was *not* fired from that job and I don't care if they call it artistic differences—our contract was good, so we're due full payment. . . . Yes, I'd be delighted to speak at the Youth Correctional Center Career Day again. I just love visiting there. They have great energy."

Irene pulled the phone away from her ear and turned to Molly. "Does Our Lady of Mercy have Career Day, petunia? I'd be more than happy to come back and give a presentation. I think hearing from a positive female role model would be very beneficial to the students. I'm an entrepreneur *and* a single parent. Tell me, is it admirable to be old, too? Because then I'd have a hat trick."

"I think today pretty much takes care of your responsibility to the students of this school, Irene," Molly answered.

"Well, maybe you're right, scooter, I wouldn't want to wear out my welcome." Irene turned her attention back to the phone. "Val, you lost me, hon. I stopped listening awhile back. . . . No, don't worry about that. You always get three threatening letters before they turn off the lights." She winked knowingly at Molly. "And, besides, you can come stay with us for a while. . . . Okay, then, I'll check in again later. *Ciao, bella.*"

"I didn't know Valerie was Italian, Molly," Mary Bridget said.

"She's from Cleveland, but Irene has been listening to that learn-to-speak-Italian tape at the office recently. She's practicing with Val."

Irene clicked off the phone, reattached it to her belt and glanced at the clock.

"We're almost out of time here, but you've really got the hang of poetry slams. Remember, good is not important. Sometimes honest is not worth that much either. But enthusiasm is always a good thing!"

The bell rang, and Irene skipped out of the room, her arm around Kyle's shoulders, without so much as a backward glance at Molly.

Molly muttered to herself as she tried to yank Irene's bag out from under her. The straps were caught on the bookshelf under her chair. She dropped to her hands and knees to free the bag. From her position on the floor, she saw Mary Bridget's loafers make their way to her row and stop.

"Thanks for taking my cello, Mol. Carolyn's dad is taking us to dance class and it won't fit in his old convertible. And the other Marys refuse to carry it for me again after that blizzard incident last winter. Although I just know that if Pats hadn't dragged her feet at her locker, they wouldn't have missed the bus and they'd have made it home with plenty of time to spare before the snow started falling that hard. Okay, gotta run. I'll swing by your house later and pick it up. Mrs. Flynn invited me for dinner. We're having leftover finger food from that party she threw to celebrate Jiffy the bear's new job."

Molly watched Mary Bridget's loafers scurry from the room. She slowly rose to her feet and glared at the cello case. She bent over, took hold of the strap and slung it over her shoulder. She straightened carefully, testing the weight. It might just be possible. She seemed to be bent a little at the knees, but if she was careful and balanced the purse just right it might not break her back. She gently pulled the purse to her, ducked her free shoulder under the straps and, taking a deep breath, slowly rose to her full height, exhaling when the weight of both the bag and the cello hit her, and trudged toward the door.

"Two more periods, that's all I have to live through," she reassured herself. "Just two more periods of school, and then soccer practice." She sighed. "Then I can run away from home."

Chapter Nine

The study of effective organizational
techniques is a must for everyone who has
something to accomplish.

—*Molly's notebook*

Mary Margaret was sitting next to Irene, reading the horoscopes in the newspaper, when Molly arrived in social studies class. "Ooh . . . I'm supposed to listen to an older, wiser person today who will give me many valuable insights," Mary Margaret announced. "You just know they mean Mrs. Flynn," she added, sighing happily. "Here's yours, Mol. 'Today is a six—'"

"Yeah," Molly said, "if one is being eaten by a shark and ten is dropping a bowling ball on your foot."

"Horoscopes are silly," Irene told Molly. "But I'd be happy to read your palm. I ordered a do-it-yourself fortune-telling kit from the back of a magazine last year, and if I do say so myself, I'm very good."

"You told me I was destined to marry a Gypsy and travel the world in a cart pulled by a pig," Molly reminded her as she dropped Mary Bridget's cello and Irene's purse to the floor and sank into her seat, rubbing her shoulders. My arms, she thought, have lost all feeling.

"What can I say?" Irene shrugged. "I see fascinating adventures in your future."

Father Connery entered the room as the bell rang and headed straight for Irene. He took both of her hands in his and grinned down at her.

"I heard you were here today. You're the buzz of the school. Irene, my good friend, I haven't seen you since you outbid me for that Boston cream pie at the silent auction during last year's Spring Fling fund-raiser."

"I've got a mean sweet tooth, Jim, and more disposable income than you."

Mary Margaret looked at Molly and mouthed, "Jim?"

Molly rolled her eyes and whispered, "Father Connery arranges all those senior citizen trips Irene takes. He's the priest she dared to try bullfighting when she went to Spain three years ago."

"You never told me the priest in the bullfighting story was Father Connery, though."

"I try to forget as much as I can about the things Irene tells me."

"Open your books to chapter eleven and we'll review the electoral college for the test next week," Father Connery said.

Irene reached over and grabbed her purse from under Molly's desk. She pulled out a radio with a headset and busily adjusted the frequency.

Father Connery glanced over. "A little mood music to help you concentrate on the finer points of democracy in action, Irene?"

"Nope, just the starting lineup for the baseball game. Cubs and Braves at Wrigley."

"Who are the starting pitchers?" he asked. "If there's a stiff breeze blowing infield this afternoon, you know it'll be a pitchers' duel."

"Don't let me disrupt your class, Jim. I'll keep the

volume low, and given how long those umpires let the at-bats drag out, I should be able to pay sufficient attention to your discussion, too. May I borrow a pencil?"

Father Connery smiled. "I'm flattered. You'll be taking notes on my lecture?"

"I've got a scorecard to fill out."

"I'm still trying to get enough people interested in that spring training trip to Florida, Irene. But it seems that you and I are the only members of the parish who'd rather tour the Grapefruit League than Cabo San Lucas. I heard St. Boniface has some keen baseball fans, so maybe we can work out an intrachurch trip next year." He sat on the edge of Irene's desk and thumbed through an old program she had pulled out of her bag, along with the radio and scorecard.

"Uh, excuse me, Father?" Molly interrupted.

"Yes, Molly?"

"Aren't we going to review for the test?"

"Oh, uh, yes, of course we are." He stood up reluctantly before looking back with a huge smile on his face. "Did you ever stop to think that a well-managed baseball team runs like a good government?"

Irene's head bobbed up, and most of the boys, who usually spent the period dozing, snapped to attention.

"Just think about it," Father Connery went on. "Democracy is a team effort—everyone has to pull their own weight to get the most out of our system of government. But there is a clear hierarchy. In our government, it is the judicial, the legislative and the executive branches. In baseball, it is the coaching staff, the general manager and the owner."

Irene continued the train of thought Father Connery had begun. "Baseball is the greatest game on earth for that reason: it is the most like our government. Neither is perfect, but both are always interesting. Baseball and democracy may not be ideal, but they are the best we have to offer. Winston Churchill said democracy was the worst form of government in the world, except for all the rest. The same might be said of baseball."

"And that's"—Irene blew a huge pink bubblegum bubble—"why baseball players get the big bucks and the beautiful babes." She shuffled through a deck of baseball cards, tucking some into a plastic bag and tossing others to a corner of her desk.

"Mrs. Flynn has the best baseball card collection of anyone I know," Mary Margaret told Father Connery.

"I don't *collect* them. I just buy them and put them on my piano in little plastic cases. I'm not a fanatic, Mary Pat."

"Mary Margaret."

"Whatever."

Father Connery opened a drawer in his desk and pulled out a clock radio. "Let's all listen to the game. Can you find the station for us, Irene, while I draw a scorecard on the blackboard?"

Mary Margaret tossed Molly a note: Don't your grandmother and Father Connery make a cute couple?!

Molly looked over at them; they were reenacting the most recent play of the game for the non-baseball fans in the class, illustrating the virtues of an ideally executed sacrifice bunt. Irene was holding a yardstick that had been abandoned in the corner of the room, using it to show how the bat catches the ball, making it bounce weakly into the infield. And Father Connery was playing the role of the befuddled infielder scrambling after the ball.

Molly scribbled a fast reply and hurled the note back to Mary Margaret. No, you boob. He's a priest. Haven't you been paying attention during religion class?

Irene was then demonstrating for three boys the proper grasp for a knuckleball as Father Connery sketched an aerial view of the infield on the blackboard.

Mary Margaret threw note after note at Molly's desk. Molly studiously ignored them all, concentrating fiercely on her textbook.

Mary Margaret resorted to whispering. "Well, I was just thinking that, since Mrs. Flynn doesn't seem to like my great-uncle Charlie, even though it's the talk of the neighborhood how stuck on her he is, maybe Father is more her type."

Without thinking, Molly blurted out, "Are you insinuating that my grandmother is flirting with a priest?"

The room fell instantly silent, and Molly looked up to see Irene crouched on the floor in a catcher's squat, flashing hand signals to the small crowd that had gathered around her. Irene ducked her head modestly and fluttered her eyelashes at Molly.

"Thanks, cutie, I'm glad to see you think this old lady still has what it takes to catch a man's eye. But"—she shook her head—"I could never flirt with someone like Father Connery." She paused. "We're just too radically different in our philosophies. For instance, he thinks the designated hitter is a good idea."

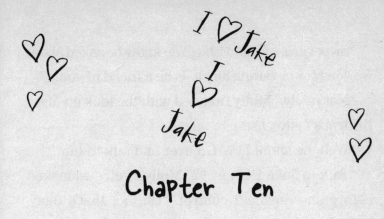

I ♡ Jake
I ♡ Jake

Chapter Ten

—*Molly's notebook*

Irene took a good look around the industrial arts workshop when they arrived at what Molly was relieved to note was the final class period. Molly did her involuntary visual sweep of the room to locate Jake Dempsey.

"Who's that?" Irene caught Molly's glance around the room and pointed to Jake. "He's a dish."

"N-n-no one," Molly stammered, feeling her cheeks turn hot and putting her hand over Irene's pointing finger. "J-just someone named Jake."

"Sweet pea, he's adorable. You know he asked about working for us during lunch. Is he a friend of yours?"

"Not really." Molly fidgeted with the lock on Mary Bridget's cello case.

"Well, he should be. Go over and talk to him."

"Talk to Jake Dempsey?" Molly's voice squeaked before she regained control. "Uh, no, that's okay, Irene."

"Oh . . . well, I see. Never mind, then." Irene whistled to herself and followed Molly to her workbench. "Whatcha doing?" she asked.

"Making a desk organizer. See, I can put my pens and pencils in this cup, I can fit a ruler in this slot thing, and this little depression is for paper clips. I'm going to add a paper tray and some little stand-up dividers for envelopes later." Molly felt content for the first time all day.

She was soon lost in the job of sanding the top of her desk organizer and checking the straightness of its edge with the mini-T-square she carried on her key chain. She'd half noticed that Irene had strolled away from her and was investigating various projects around the room.

Molly was debating whether to add a magnet to the paper clip tray when she began to hear fragments of an argument drifting her way from across the room. At first she didn't pay attention. But when she heard Irene's raised voice, she looked up and dropped her sanding block.

Her grandmother was standing on a box, which made her tall enough to peer down at the innards of an engine that were scattered across a workbench. She was standing next to Jake Dempsey.

Jake and Irene were talking. Not just talking, but arguing. Loudly.

". . . so you want to retard the timing on the compression stroke to set more power," Irene said.

"Yeah, if you *want* to ruin the engine." Jake frowned at the engine part he held in his hand.

"Anyone who knows the principles of an internal combustion engine—"

Irene caught Molly's eye.

"Flowerpot, come over here."

Molly shook her head vigorously.

Irene beckoned again.

Molly shook her head again. As much as she wanted to run from the room or disappear completely, she was unable to turn away from the sight of her grandmother and Jake working together.

Irene got a glint in her eye and picked up a booklet from the workbench, waving it in Molly's direction.

"There's a manual," she called. "Just full of instructions and directions and, um, rules and regulations and so on and so forth."

Molly's ears pricked up. She felt her feet slowly move toward her grandmother.

Irene made room for her in front of the engine next to Jake. Molly couldn't begin to meet Jake's eyes. She took the manual from Irene with shaking hands and tried to concentrate on the words printed in it. She studied the bits of machinery scattered in front of her, trying to align them with the instructions in the manual.

"It's an outboard motor for my dad's fishing boat. I'm trying to juice it up, and your grandma is helping," Jake explained.

"That's a head gasket, right?" Molly asked, pointing. "I mean, it looks like the picture in the book."

"Yeah, that's right. Can you hand me that little screwdriver?"

"Oh, sure. And these must be spark plugs." Molly concentrated on the manual, then looked back at the parts on the workbench.

"Uh-huh," Jake said. "Are you twitching?"

"Um, sort of. I don't usually, I mean, but we had a funky lunch. Is this piece cracked or is it supposed to look like this?"

Jake took it from her hand. "Yeah, we'll have to replace it. You know, I've seen you before, but you seemed like you'd be hard to talk to."

"I, um, thought the same thing about you."

"Then I'm glad your grandma came over to see what I was doing. She's wrong about internal combustion engines, of course, but interesting to talk to."

"That's what everyone says about her. Really, I'm not very much like her. At all. Ever."

"You're kidding, right? You've got a black eye and you're twitching. And I don't know what's all over you but it smells like lunch. And you seem real cool about it all. Plus, you pick up mechanical stuff real quick. That makes you the most interesting girl I've talked to all day."

You only think that, Molly thought, because you didn't get the memo about how really boring I am. But this time, wisely, she kept her mouth shut.

Chapter Eleven

Age and treachery will always overcome youth and skill.

—*Irene*

Molly trudged back to the locker room from the field after soccer practice, squishing loudly with each step. Mary Pat jogged to catch up with her.

"Sorry about that puddle, Molly. I tried to pass the ball to your right so you'd miss it."

"That's okay, Pats. That's my blind side today. I know you didn't mean it."

"Is your grandmother coming home with us on the activity bus? Or do you think she's going to stay for the entire cheerleading practice?" Mary Pat stopped in front of her locker. "You've got to admit, she looked pretty awesome out there. I'm glad to see that Kathleen Ferguson doesn't have the highest kick on the squad after all."

Molly spun the combination on her lock and jerked it open. She stood there dumbly, waiting for the reality of what she saw, or rather what she didn't see, to sink in. Mary Pat glanced over when she noticed that Molly hadn't responded.

"My stuff . . . all my stuff is gone, Pats. First my notebook and now my clothes. I can't believe this." She stared blankly at the empty locker. "Somebody took all my clothes."

"Here, Mol." Mary Pat quickly rooted through her own locker and thrust a bundle of clothes into Molly's hands. "I have an extra school uniform you can borrow. Uh-oh, no shoes. Check the lost and found. There's sure to be something drier than those wet soccer cleats you're wearing. At least something to get you home."

Mary Pat looked past Molly and brightened.

"Look! Today's not a total waste. Your grandmother's bag and Mary Bridget's cello didn't get stolen! They're right over there in the corner where you hid them."

Molly cast a baleful glance at the cursed black bag and cello case as she sloshed her way numbly to the lost and found box on the other side of the locker room.

Ten minutes later, she was alone in the now deserted locker room, sitting silently on the bench in front of her locker, staring down at the bowling shoe on her right foot and the Rollerblade on her left foot. Our Lady of Mercy Middle School, Molly thought, has a crummy selection in their lost and found.

Everyone else had changed their clothes and quickly left the building after casting leery glances at Molly, who appeared to be in a trance. She took a deep breath, pulled herself to her feet, slung Irene's bag across her body and began the awkward thump-glide, thump-glide toward the buses outside, Mary Bridget's cello bouncing painfully off her shin with each thump-glide.

"Gimme a B! B! Gimme an A!" Irene was standing outside near the door waiting for Molly, fluffing her new pom-poms and cheering softly to herself. She stopped abruptly when she caught sight of Molly's dejected face. "Kitten, what's wrong?"

"Wrong? Why would you ask if anything's wrong, Irene?" Molly thump-glided a few feet past Irene before spinning around suddenly to face her.

"Okay, let's recap my day thus far: I lost my notebook, but I'm carrying around fifty pounds of *your* junk in the big black bag from hell, plus this cello. I couldn't have a best friend who played the harmonica, now could I, or maybe even the flute? Oh, no, Bridge has to play the heaviest instrument in the universe and I get stuck carrying it around."

Molly stopped to catch her breath. "I got a black eye and was forced to participate in a talent show, all before school even started. Not only does my grandmother insist on being the only human in the Western Hemisphere who takes Senior Citizens' Day seriously and actually comes to school, but then she gets accused of smoking in the bathroom.

"I missed science and got detention. I tore my dress up to my throat and what didn't rip got burned when one of the dysfunctional malcontents you now call a buddy set me on fire. Half of my hair is in tiny braids that are held in place by rubber bands that were in someone's mouth."

Molly paused for a moment, giving her thoughts a chance to catch up with her rapidly building fury.

"We ate lunch with a bunch of soon-to-be criminals who have probably moved into my room by now, because, in addition to giving them all jobs, I'm sure that room and board is the next offer you'll make to them."

Irene moved as if to speak, but Molly raised a hand.

"Just so you don't think the day was a total waste, I did get to talk to the cutest boy in school. Too bad that every square inch of me was covered in spaghetti sauce and blue-black ink. Oh, yeah, and I was twitching from the coffee beans we had for lunch, so he probably thinks I'm clinically insane.

"The only bad thing that *hasn't* happened to me today is that I haven't been carried off by little trolls, but, hey, the day is still young.

"And it's all because I lost my notebook." Molly was sobbing now, standing outside the locker room door. "You don't understand," she sniffled. "That notebook contained a list of all my life's goals and I'm just . . . lost without it."

"I thought you had a wonderful day, Molly."

Molly didn't even bother to respond. She just dragged her sleeve across her nose.

"In any case," Irene continued gently, "don't you think you're just a little too dependent on that notebook?"

"Well, yes, you could say that. But I can't rely on that computer diary you got me for Christmas. You know I don't have a laptop, and the success of my notebook system depends on constant access, an ongoing system of updating and refining . . ." Molly trailed off and looked up at Irene.

"Molly, Molly, Molly. Your life is much more important than what you put in that notebook." Irene grabbed her bag from where Molly had dropped it, reached in and rooted around for a moment before pulling Molly's notebook out with a flourish.

"See, I told you I could carry everything I needed in my bag," she remarked triumphantly.

Molly stared at the notebook in Irene's hand. "Did you take my clothes from the locker too?"

"Molly, I was manipulative today, not mean. Nope, that was just good old-fashioned bad luck."

"You mean I've been carrying my notebook around all day?"

"I thought that had a nice *Wizard of Oz* touch—just like Dorothy, you had what you needed all along, only you didn't know it. I took the notebook from you yesterday when I saw that you never did anything without checking it off your to-do list. I worried that you wouldn't even scratch your a—"

"Is this some kind of joke?"

Irene shook her head. "Look, Molly, this is the kind of day that builds character."

"Because if this is all some kind of sick joke, I'm not laughing." Molly studied her borrowed clothes, picking at the blouse. It didn't quite fit, she thought, like her life. "I'm done, Irene. I'm all done and fed up and sick of it all, so if there's some kind of punch line coming for this hysterically funny joke, you'd better let it fly because I'm . . . I'm done."

Irene smiled softly. "Dear one, there is no joke, only me loving you and wanting to help you. And maybe sometimes I'm a little heavy-handed and maybe sometimes it seems to go sideways a little, but the truth is that everything I am is for you, to help you. If nothing else comes from this day, I hope you at least see that."

Molly looked up, caught by the tone in Irene's voice, the softness, and felt her good eye tear up, and something inside her tore a little and all her anger left her and she reached over to throw her arms around Irene and they clasped each other tightly and stood that way for a long and wonderful time, until Molly was startled by a cheer that went up from behind them.

Looking over Irene's shoulder, she saw that their whole conversation had been closely followed by the entire membership of the detention squad, who were now hanging out the windows of the Detention Room, cheering and whooping.

Molly waved at them, gave them a thumbs-up and smiled. If you had to have new friends, she thought, they weren't so bad. It was kind of like being friendly with a bunch of pit bulls.

Chapter Twelve

Misery is optional.

—*Irene*

Irene gently pulled out of their hug and returned the notebook to Molly. She looked over Molly's shoulder at the activity bus and got a crafty gleam in her eyes.

"You'd better hurry if you want to catch that bus, Mol."

"Aren't you coming home with me?" Molly asked.

"I'll be home in a bit. But I have a date with the padre for pie. I'm going to try to convince that social studies teacher of yours how wrong he is about the infield fly rule." Irene jogged off, pom-poms fluttering, to find Father Connery.

The driver stopped Molly as she started up the steps.

"No blades on the bus."

"That's okay, I'll hop."

Molly lifted the foot with the Rollerblade and, using the cello as a crutch, boarded the bus. She ignored the astonished faces that silently turned as she made her way toward the only available seat, which was, she noted with a small shiver, next to Jake.

She sat down and sighed as she let Mary Bridget's cello case drop to the floor of the bus with a gratifying crash. She grinned at all the heads that swiveled toward her.

"It's a cello," she called cheerfully. She turned, still smiling, to Jake. "It's Mary Bridget's cello and I'm taking it home for her."

"Nice blade," he commented, studying her carefully.

"Thanks. I found it. Nicer wheels than my own pair. Of course, I have two of those."

"You look like you've had a rough day."

She looked down at her feet and thoughtfully tapped the bowling shoe and the Rollerblade together. Then she looked up at herself in the convex mirror at the front of the bus: tiny braids on one side, black eye on the other, a smudge of blue-black ink on her cheek.

"Actually, it turned out to be a really good day," she said, smiling at her reflection.

"Cool," Jake said, touching her hand. "Totally cool."

About the Author

Gary Paulsen is the distinguished author of many critically acclaimed books for young people, including three Newbery Honor books: *The Winter Room*, *Hatchet* and *Dogsong*. His novel *The Haymeadow* received the Western Writers of America Golden Spur Award. Among his Random House books are *The Glass Café; How Angel Peterson Got His Name; Caught by the Sea; Guts: The True Stories Behind* Hatchet *and the Brian Books; The Beet Fields; Alida's Song* (a companion to *The Cookcamp*); *Soldier's Heart; The Transall Saga; My Life in Dog Years; Sarny: A Life Remembered* (a companion to *Nightjohn*); *Brian's Return, Brian's Winter* and *Brian's Hunt* (companions to *Hatchet*); *Father Water, Mother Woods;* and five books about Francis Tucket's adventures in the Old West. Gary Paulsen has also published fiction and nonfiction for adults, as well as picture books illustrated by his wife, the painter Ruth Wright Paulsen. Their most recent book is *Canoe Days*. The Paulsens live in New Mexico and on the Pacific Ocean.